Throne Spirits

Ellie Abood
and
Aashna Kshirsagar

PUBLISHED BY

SIGMA'S
BOOKSHELF

MINNETONKA, MN 55305
WWW.SIGMASBOOKSHELF.COM

Dedications

I am dedicating this book to my parents. They always support me with everything I do. I also dedicate this book to my little sister Emily. She is the sweetest person I know. Also thanks to Mrs. Bernard, our Language Arts teacher. She helped us with our writing and came up with good ideas. Thank you to Dr. Rodgers and Mr. Newman, who encouraged us along the way. Lastly, thanks to my friends who always make me smile!

~ Ellie Abood

I am dedicating this book to my parents who encourage me and are always there for me. I would also like to dedicate this book to my friends who are there to make me laugh. Lastly, I want to dedicate this book to our librarian, Dr. Rodgers, our homeroom teacher, Mr. Newman, and our Language Arts teacher, Mrs. Bernard, who helped us through this process.

~ Aashna Kshirsagar

Prologue

Years ago in the far off land of Linston, there was a little princess. Her name was Claire Monakean. She was a cute one, but being cute and adorable wasn't the only side of her. Trust me, she was a pain in the neck. She still is now—at the age of seventeen.

I'm McKenna Monakean and unfortunately I'm her little sister. I'm fourteen-years-old. I don't see how she got picked by our parents to live on as the next generation of being Queen! Even though I'm younger, and as our parents think "less mature," I think I should be able to be the Queen. For all of my life, I have been treated badly by Claire. She is so ANNOYING! When she is Queen, she might just take over the world, and I don't want to be her slave.

Once, when we were younger, my sister and I both wanted some chocolate milk. Unfortunately, there was only one serving left, so we resolved our issues with a serious game of rock, paper, scissors. I won fair and square, but before I could get the milk, she dashed over and drank it all to the very last drop. I was so mad at her I could have screamed!

Although I thought she was a big dum-dum everyone else thought she was very intelligent. She got an A+ in all of her royal classes, even psychology. I only got an A-, and the occasional and more likely B. We don't need to go over the one F in reading. One time when Claire got an A she cried because it wasn't an A+.

Her life is so rainbows and unicorns and my life is just bleh, although I do have a few million dollars worth of wardrobe, jewelry and more. The whole village thinks she is going to be a good Queen—somehow, and that's just what might happen.

Claire is seventeen now and it's the year of her coronation. I can't believe she is going to be crowned Queen soon.

Chapter 1

Midnight Breeze

One late Friday night, I was walking through the castle looking for a midnight snack when I heard a noise. It just sounded like a strong gust of wind, so I ignored it. By the time I opened the fridge, I felt a breeze on my neck. I grabbed an apple then quickly turned around, but nothing was there. I hesitated then walked away. I still felt something wasn't quite right, but I knew that I could handle some silly wind.

I walked up the stairs to my bedroom. I shut the door and closed the windows and drapes, in case a storm was coming. I got in my bed and turned out the lights. Around 1:00 a.m., I woke up when someone opened the door. I thought it was probably just my mom, so I sat up. WOW —my room was a mess. Clothes were on the floor, my jewelry was spilled and my closet was a disaster! So I got out of bed, grabbed my flashlight, and went outside my room.

"Hello?" I said as my words echoed throughout the castle hallway. As I expected, no one answered. *It must be a storm, right? What else could it be?*

Just in case, I called out again, but still no answer. I walked down the steps toward the kitchen—maybe someone is downstairs. When I got to the bottom step, I saw a shadow and felt something go through me as I started to get very woozy.

"Wait, what's happening?" I whispered as my face was going pale. "You-you're a ghost!" I said.

The shadow became less transparent. I started to see a human-like creature. At that point, I bolted in the other direction. The shadow then started chasing me. I heard something coming from the staircase. I thought it was another ghost, but it wasn't. It was Claire, my snotty, bratty, over confident older sister. She ran toward the thing with a flashlight and hit it over the head. Thankfully, it scattered away.

She ran to me and said, "McKenna, are you okay?" I was shocked. Usually, Claire never said anything nice to me.

"Yeah. How did you know to save me?"

"When I heard someone scream like a little girl, I had to see what was going on," she said.

That's the Claire I expected—she's back.

"But when I heard and saw it was you, I had to help."

"Thanks."

"No problem," she said with a grin.

"Claire, by the way, do you think the ghost looked familiar at all?"

"No, why?" she asked.

"Never mind."

I had an empty feeling in the bottom of my stomach. I knew something was wrong.

After Claire "saved" me from the ghost—I decided that I'm going to call whatever it was a ghost—we both headed our separate ways to bed. I tried to sleep, but I was too restless. I stayed awake all night staring at the ceiling thinking about what had happened and all the possibilities. I don't know when, but sometime around 5:00 a.m., I finally fell asleep. I guess I was tired because when I woke up it was 2:00 p.m. I decided to forget about what had happened the previous night and take some time to relax. The day turned out great. Claire didn't talk to me about what had happened at all and I didn't talk to her. It was as if nothing had happened. The day went completely normal. Unfortunately, that wasn't the case at night.

I was embarrassed to admit it, but I was kind of scared to go to sleep. *Don't be a baby,* I thought to myself. *What you saw was some sort of an illusion, ghosts aren't real!*

Chapter 2

Ghosts Aren't
Real (I Hope)

As I was just starting to fall asleep, I heard muffled sounds in the hallway. The ballroom was right down the hall from my room, so I could hear every little sound that echoed from any corner of the room. The ballroom door screeched open, and slammed shut quickly. Then I heard the piano being played. I quickly leaped out of my bed and grabbed the nearest weapon to me—a hairbrush! *Hey, if Claire can use a flashlight I can use a hairbrush.* I quietly crept into the ballroom to see what was going on. I opened the door very slowly, but in true shock and surprise, it was Claire.

"Claire?! What are you doing here?" I asked her with great confusion.

"Here? Oh yeah I was just looking around the castle," she said speaking super fast.

"You've lived here for seventeen years now. Why do you choose to look around now? Also, please can you 'look around' another time because if you haven't noticed, people are trying to sleep!"

"Okay, okay if you have to know," she said.

"Know what?" I asked suspiciously.

"That I was the one playing piano because I'm nervous

about my speech at school in History class, but don't tell anyone," she told me, sounding a bit embarrassed.

"Okay, but you really scared me. I thought it was that ghost again!" I said.

"Oh my gosh McKenna. There are no more ghosts. Remember, I saved you by knocking it out with my flashlight. Besides, it was probably just a windy night with fog, and it was at like two in the morning. You were probably seeing things anyway."

"Are you sure? That ghost seemed pretty real," I said skeptically.

"I am positive it was not real."

"Oh really? I'll bet you a day's worth of allowance, one hundred dollars, that the ghost was real."

"Okay."

Just then the door squeaked open and we both jumped up in surprise.

"Phew," I said to myself under my breath. It was only Henry, our royal guard and one of our family's closest friends. He was looking pretty tired in his pajamas, and for some reason he had a huge bruise on his forehead.

"Henry? What are you doing? Are you spying on us?" Claire questioned him rudely with a lot of sass.

"I'm sorry, your highness. There was such a racket in here I thought someone had broken in!" he said politely, unlike Claire.

"Oh, whoops," Claire said, now embarrassed as her cheeks grew red.

"By the way, what's up with that huge bruise on your forehead?" Claire asked, again very rudely.

"I just slipped and fell pretty hard." You could tell by the look on his face that he had been asked that question multiple times today.

"C'mon Claire, let's go," I said as Henry started to leave.

"Okay, but first I want to grab a snack. I'm kind of hungry, want to come with me?"

I was super thirsty and a little hungry so I said, "Sure."

As we headed to the kitchen, shivers went down my spine as I found myself thinking about the ghost from yesterday.

"Ahhhhh," Claire fake screamed.

"What?" I asked Claire very annoyed. Claire overreacts to everything. Once I was wearing a dark brown shirt and purple sweat pants and she screamed when she saw me because it was such an "ugly" combination.

"McKenna look over there," she said to me in a mocking tone. "It's a ghost."

"No, it's a white blanket over a coat hanger," I said rolling my eyes.

Then she came up behind me and said, "Boo!"

"Ha ha, very funny," I said sarcastically. "Let's go get something to eat."

In the kitchen, Claire teased me nonstop about the ghost. Again, like yesterday, as I opened the door of the fridge, I felt air blow on my neck. This time I didn't bother to turn around because I knew it was Claire.

"Stop it Claire," I said getting very frustrated by now.

"Okay, fine."

As we headed out of the kitchen all I was thinking about was how angry I was at Claire. *Sometimes Claire can be so annoying*, I thought to myself. Suddenly, I felt another cool breeze that sent shivers down my spine. This time I knew it wasn't Claire because she was standing in front of me. *That's odd*, I thought, so I turned around only to see—the ghost again!

Now that I think about it, I'm surprised I didn't scream! Instead, I slowly tapped Claire on the shoulder and quietly whispered, "Claire the ghost is behind you. Turn around slowly."

"Yeah right. You just want to get me back for teasing you earlier."

"No. I swear. I'm one hundred percent serious." I must have sounded very serious and scared because she did turn around.

"Okay fine...Ahhhhhhhhhhhhhhhhhhhhhhhh," she screamed so loud it could have woken up the paintings! After she screamed, the ghost, like the last time, scattered away as if it was afraid of the noise Claire was making. Next, I heard feet running in the distance coming closer to where we were.

"What's the matter your highness?" asked one of the guards, Alex, on night duty.

"There was a ghost!" I said to him.

"Yes there was! That's why I screamed!" said Claire.

The guard looked very doubtful, but he said, "Okay, are you safe?"

"Yeah, we're fine now," Claire replied.

"I will walk you back to your rooms," said the guard. I didn't like the fact that he was "walking" us back to our rooms. It made me feel like a little kid, but then again, it also felt safer.

After I settled into bed, I was afraid the ghost would come and attack me or haunt me. Now that I think about it, today the ghost appeared in the exact same spot it did yesterday. Thankfully, the ghost didn't appear again that night. I fell asleep pretty quickly because I was still tired from the "attack" that happened the day before. My eyes slowly fluttered before they finally closed shut and my day ended.

Chapter 3

Ghosts Are Real (I'm Sure)

In the morning, as soon as I woke up (around 8:00), I went to Claire's room to talk about the ghost and claim my one hundred dollars. As I walked over to Claire's room, I avoided the spot in the hallway where we saw the ghost. It took me twice the amount of time to go out of my way, but I'm not taking any chances. I don't want to see that ghost again.

When I got to Claire's room, she was in her bathroom brushing her teeth. "Claire?"

"Phh mph mph" she said, her mouth full of toothpaste and water.

"Huh?" I asked her. "I didn't understand a thing you just said."

After gargling, she asked me, "What do you want?"

"Well, first of all, I want my one hundred dollars. Remember our bet? You said if the ghost we saw was real, you would hand over one hundred dollars!"

"Okay fine," she said while grumbling. She almost never loses bets. She reached in her pocket and pulled out a fresh one hundred dollar bill and handed it to me. She started to storm out of her room, but before she could leave, I said, "Wait, Claire!"

"What?" she replied back obviously still mad about the bet.

"I need to talk to you about the ghost," I told her.

"What's there to talk about? It's simple. There's a ghost haunting us, I think."

"Yes! You believe me! This calls for a celebration! Cupcakes, on you!"

"What do you mean? You just got one hundred dollars and I still have to pay?"

"Yup! Meet me at 10:00 p.m. in your room for cupcakes! Remember to get my two favorites: red velvet and strawberry banana whipped cream."

"First of all, NOT MY ROOM! Also, I'm only getting you one cupcake!"

"Fine, but I could tell all your friends that you believe in ghosts!"

"Uh, okay fine. My room and two cupcakes," said Claire.

"See you later!" I said victoriously. When leaving Claire's room, like before, I avoided the spot where we saw the ghost.

Later that night, I was so excited when it was time for cupcakes. "I'm coming for my cupcakes!" I said with great joy as I made my way to Claire's room. "I can't wait to—"

I suddenly heard a scream that sounded just like Claire. It was coming from her room. "AHHHHHH! The-The-The GHOST!"

I started to run toward her room. I hoped I wouldn't be too late. *That's odd,* I thought to myself. *I don't hear any noise now. I hope Claire is okay.*

I finally made it to her room and shoved the door open just in time to see the ghost scatter away, like the last two times. I couldn't catch my breath, as I was panting from running so fast.

"What did you do that for?" Claire shouted at me. "You scared the ghost away!"

"What do you mean? I saved you!" I replied back very confused.

"No you didn't! The ghost was starting to talk to me! It was just about to tell me why it was here!" she said, sounding very mad.

"Oh whoops," I said sheepishly. "So, did it say anything to you?"

"Only one thing—Library."

Chapter 4

Putting the Pieces Together

"Library! What is that supposed to mean?" I questioned.

"How should I know? Maybe it means that we should read more books?" Claire replied unsure.

"I'm pretty sure it doesn't mean we should read more," I said confidently. "One hundred percent sure."

"How would you know? You got an F in reading class! You just stopped reading overall after that."

"First of all, that F was in Kindergarten. Second, I didn't stop reading, I only minimized it!"

"Oh really?" Claire asked. "When was the last time you read a book?"

"Yesterday! It was a book about this little girl who wore a red hood."

"I think you mean Little Red Riding Hood!"

"Oh yeah, that book," I said.

"Anyway, when was the last time you read a real book, a chapter book?" Claire continued to inquire.

"Um, three years ago, I think. So, not too long ago."

"Wow, your definition of 'not too long ago' is way different from mine."

"Wait, I think I know what it means!" I exclaimed.

"Says the girl who hasn't read a REAL BOOK IN THREE YEARS!" Claire exclaimed.

"I think the ghost is trying to tell us to go to the library."

"Why would we need to go to the library?"

"Maybe clues will be there," I said.

"Maybe, but I doubt it," Claire said.

"Be positive! Or else I could text your friends about this whole little scenario and they'll probably have a good laugh—at you!" I threatened.

"Okay, fine. We can go to the library tomorrow."

"Why not tonight?"

"Have you not realized that it's past ten o'clock? The library will be closed, plus there's something called SLEEP! Also, what do you think Mom and Dad will say when they find out that we are looking for 'ghosts' late at night?"

"Ugh fine, but I still want my cupcakes!" I told Claire.

I quickly ate my two amazing cupcakes and rushed to my bedroom. When I reached my room, I changed into pajamas and got myself tucked into bed. As I laid there, I started to plan out, in my head, what we were going to do tomorrow morning at the library. We should get up early in the morning around 6:00 a.m. Well, at least I would. Usually, I was the early riser and Claire was the late riser. Her definition of getting up early was 10:30a.m.

After I get Claire to wake up, we should go to the library to hunt for clues, I thought to myself. I imagined us finding clues that would lead us from one place to another, like a fun scavenger hunt!

In the morning, I was so excited that I woke up at 5:45 a.m. and got ready in just five minutes! I skipped over to Claire's room and knocked on the door. When no one answered, I decided to go in. Claire was still sleeping. She was snoring, but very softly. So I debated what to do:

Option one: Quietly try to wake her up with a little shake.

Option two: Scream "WAKE UP" at the top of my lungs, guaranteeing that she will wake up.

Option three: Jump on her bed, which will make her eventually get up, plus I get to have a little fun.

Option four: Pour cold water on her face.

Option five: Tickle her on her neck and feet.

I immediately ruled out option one because that would be no fun for me. Then I definitely ruled out option two because I didn't want to wake up anyone else in the castle, besides Claire. I finally decided on option four.

I left Claire's room quickly to fetch a cup. I tried to fill it up with the coldest water I could find. I was walking over to her and I was just about to throw the water on her face when she woke up and saw me! My mistake. I was being too loud. I didn't expect Claire to wake up because of a little noise. She is usually a very heavy sleeper.

"McKenna, what are you do—?"

Then out of nowhere, my instincts told me to throw the cup of water on her face, so I did. It's like my arm had a mind of its own! Soaked and very cold, Claire angrily said, "WHAT WAS THAT FOR?"

"Sorry. I was just trying to wake you up," I said, kind of afraid of what she was going to do to me.

"WAKE ME UP? I was already awake!"

"Sorry?"

"Not helping! Anyway, why are you trying to wake me up at, I don't know 6:00 a.m.?"

"So that we could go to the library," I said very quietly under my breath.

"You know we could have just gone to the library at Noon, like normal people!" Claire said, still very mad.

"We could, but that wouldn't be as exciting!" I said while mimicking her in my head!

"OH NO!"

"What, what is it?" I replied back.

"YOU ARE WEARING A BROWN T-SHIRT AND PURPLE OVERALLS! IF YOU DON'T CHANGE NOW, I WON'T GO TO THE LIBRARY!"

"Okay, I'll go change into a purple t-shirt, with brown overalls," I said very amused.

"MCKENNA!"

"Ugh! Fine. I'll wear something 'nice.'"

"What is your definition of 'nice' because that would be interesting to know?"

"Ha ha, let me get ready, again! I'll meet you at the royal vehicle in thirty minutes, you know, so you have some time to dry off. Tootles!"

"Ugh, you are so annoying," Claire muttered.

Chapter 5

Library of Clues

While Claire dried off, I changed into some "nicer" clothes. I then headed to my parents' bedroom to ask permission to go to the library. Unfortunately, they told me that I could only go if I was wearing a royal gown. Ugh, another changing session. There is a rule that whenever I go outside the castle, I have to wear one of my royal gowns. My parents always want me to look perfect for the people. When I am in the castle, I can wear whatever I want, even if Claire doesn't approve! My parents also said that I need to have Claire "supervise" me at the library. Good thing she was already coming! I'm so glad she wasn't here for this talk. I don't want her aware that she is my "supervisor". Unfortunately, once I got to the royal vehicle, I found out she had previously talked to our parents and already knew about the "supervisor" role.

When we started to pull away, Claire rudely said, "Get comfortable princess, as for the next few hours, I'm your Queen!"

What's great about being a princess is when you pass people on the streets, they always bow to you. Plus, you don't have to work at all! When you're the Queen, you have loads of hard work, while the princess (a.k.a. me) does whatever she pleases whenever she pleases to do so. Unless her parents say differently.

When we approached the library, I was amazed at how many books it had. There were more than ten whole chapter books! That's more than I could read in a lifetime. To be honest, they probably had three thousand books! Only a true lame-o (Claire) would read that many books. *I can't wait to find clues! Claire and I are going to have so much fun,* I thought to myself.

"So what's your plan?" Claire asked me.

"How should I know? You're the 'supervisor,'" I replied being a bit snotty.

"What do you mean? I thought you had a plan!" Claire exclaimed.

"Nope."

"Ughhhh fine. Maybe we should just look around to see if we can find anything interesting or suspicious."

"Okay," I said.

Claire and I both headed our separate ways. I had absolutely no idea what I was looking for and where in the library it would be!

"Oooo, a puppet show!" I said out loud to myself. I quickly rushed over there before it started. It was actually pretty interesting. I knew most of the storyline because it was about the same book I had read a few days ago—Riding Hood Red, at least I think that's what it was called. Oh, now I remember. It was called Red Hood Riding.

In the middle of the puppet show, I got a call on my cell phone. I decided to ignore it because it was getting to a really interesting part in the show, but it rang again. This time I picked it up just in case it was an emergency. As I expected, it was only Claire.

"What do you want?" I asked Claire, very annoyed that she made me miss the most important part of the show.

"Where are you?" she asked me.

"The real question is, where are you? Why aren't you watching the puppet show with me? You're supposed to be my supervisor, so why aren't you supervising?"

"Wait a second. Did you just tell me you've been watching a puppet show for the last hour while I've been looking for clues everywhere?"

"No, I was uh, doing this, uh, thing," I replied back. Even I could tell that it was a very bad lie.

"Doing what thing?" she asked me.

"I'm uh, reading a book."

"Oh really? And what book would that be?"

I quickly glanced around to see if there were any books around for me to say I was reading. Unfortunately, the closest book to me was "The History of Cement." So I said, "I'm reading 'The History of Cement.'"

"Yeah, I highly doubt that and also how does that help us? Ghosts and cement are two completely different things!" she said angrily and confused.

"Okay, okay, fine. I was watching the puppet show," I confessed.

"Did you learn anything? Were there any clues in the show?"

"Well, I learned to never trust talking wolves!"

"Seriously, that's what you learned?"

"Yup."

"Oh my gosh. You are completely useless."

"Sorry," I said not actually meaning it.

"Okay. Now instead of just doing nothing, please do something that's actually useful!"

"Okay, okay. I'll go look for clues."

Before I went to search for clues, I waited until the show was over. Sadly, I didn't really understand the ending because Claire had so rudely interrupted my viewing. At first, I just strolled around the library, but then I decided to actually try to look for something. The librarian offered to give me a complete tour of the library, but I said no. I didn't know what to look for, but then I remembered all the movies I'd seen with cool trap doors. Usually the main character leaned against a shelf or something, and then a trap door would open! So I decided to lean on a bookshelf very casually. Unfortunately, instead of a secret trap door opening the entire bookshelf fell down! The librarian and about ten other people, including Claire, rushed over to where I was quietly standing, very embarrassed.

"Princess, are you okay?" asked some townsfolk.

"What in the world happened here?" asked Claire full of surprise.

"Uh, I might have accidentally knocked down a bookshelf."

"MIGHT HAVE?" Claire exclaimed. "What were you thinking?"

"Okay, okay, I was leaning against the bookshelf so that a secret trap door would pop open!"

"Stuff like that only happens in movies," said Claire.

"Well, how was I supposed to know that? I'm getting bored. Let's go home," I complained, trying to avoid a lecture about how foolish that was.

"Already? We've barely been here for two hours and we haven't found anything yet!"

By now I could tell she was getting very annoyed and very angry.

"Okay, fine. I guess we can stay here until we find something helpful," I said.

"Thank you," Claire replied still sounding mad.

We both headed our separate ways again. I felt kind of bad for the librarian who had to pick up all those books I had dropped. When she took a break, I decided to help out a bit. As I was shelving the books, one of them caught my eye.

"The Map of Linston," I whispered out loud to myself.

I decided that it might be helpful, so I flipped through the book. As I was ruffling through the pages, I stopped at one page because it was slightly bent. The heading on the top of the page read, "The Linston Library." I realized that this didn't seem to be the same library I was standing in right now. This looked like it was in the exact same spot as the abandoned building I passed on my way to school everyday. I read a little bit more of the chapter. Apparently, I was right. It used to be the Linston Library, but for some reason they built a new one—the one I was standing in right now!

Suddenly, it dawned on me. The library I was reading about was the one the ghost was talking about. The ghost must want Claire and I to go to the old library for some reason. I called Claire over to tell her what I had found.

"Look! The ghost wanted us to go to the old Linston Library!"

"Huh?" Claire questioned.

"The abandoned building on the way to school!"

"You're right!" she exclaimed "The ghost was probably talking about the old library!"

"Wow, you think I'm right? Say that again. I want to get that on tape!" I exclaimed, surprised that she thought I was right for once.

"Anyway, I think we should go to the old library to see if we find anything interesting," Claire said.

"Okay," I replied back.

"How about tomorrow?" Claire asked.

"Can we do the day after? I think I'm going to sleep in tomorrow."

"Okay," Claire replied back.

She turned around to leave, but then she said, "Just don't go without me. We're in this together."

Chapter 6

The Hunt Back to 1823

At night, I didn't sleep well. I had nightmares of the ghost attacking me. At 4:06 a.m., I opened my eyes as I woke up sweaty and scared from the nightmare. I decided to try and go back to sleep, but there was a zero percent chance of that happening. So I just laid there until my alarm rang at 7:45a.m.

When I finally got up, I pondered if I should go to the library alone. I knew that Claire would get mad if I went by myself, but I just had to know today. The anxiousness was killing me! I finally came to the decision that I would go without Claire. I had no choice. If I woke her up now, she would be really crabby. I quickly ate breakfast and I asked my Dad if I could take a "walk" around the kingdom. He said yes, but as always, I needed to wear my gown. Another changing session. This is getting pretty old now.

While I was walking up and down the streets of Linston, I saw the abandoned Linston Library. At least I think it was abandoned. The building was a burgundy color with a layer of dust covering all the walls. There was also a "closed" sign hanging from the window frame. I had driven past the building so many times and barely glanced at it. Now looking at it up close, it seemed very odd.

I walked up to the window and wiped off some dust.

I only saw a chair or two, but mostly books surrounded the room. I was pondering if I should walk in when, out of nowhere, the door shot open. It felt like it was calling me. It was really scary, but exciting. I stopped to think if I should go back and wait for Claire, but I walked in anyway, not thinking about my future.

As I walked through the door, it made a screeching sound on the floor. It was all dusty, like the outside of the building. There was no one in sight. However, there was a soft chair with a piece of a crumpled up newspaper on it. As I walked over toward the dusty purple chair, I suddenly saw an old man sitting around the corner.

"Who are you?" I asked him, shocked and with some fear.

He mumbled something.

I curiously said, "Speak up!"

He mumbled again, but I understood it this time. He said, "Read this, it will help you."

"How do you know what I'm looking for?" I asked in complete shock.

"Just read it!"

That kind of gave me the feeling I should read it.

The headline said, "Our King is Missing!"

"That wasn't the front page article this week! It was about some school bake sale!"

"Look at the date."

"Oh," I said.

It read, "December 8, 1823." That was almost two hundred years ago! There was also a picture in the newspaper. It was of the King before he went missing—forever.

"Who are you?"

He replied back, "Let's just say I'm family."

"Family of who?"

Before he could tell me anything more, he vanished into thin air.

Then I heard a whisper "Jeremy. Jeremy Monakean!"

Suddenly, I saw a greenish gas flowing from one side of the room. I only remember falling and the newspaper flying out the window. Everything else faded away.

Chapter 7

Hospital

I woke up in an unfamiliar place. I felt confused and woozy as I sat up in the bed. Someone walked in and stood next to me. My vision was very off, but I still recognized her. She started speaking, but it was very hard to comprehend what she was saying.

To my great surprise, I heard her scream my name as loud as possible. It was like a crazy woman thinking I would hear her only if she yells. How rude! My vision started unfogging, but the "crazy person" who was screaming my name was clearly my seventeen-year-old sister. Seventeen! Like who does that! Claire I guess.

"Why the heck are you screaming in my face?" I asked.

"Because you're a royal LIAR!"

"Liar! What are you talking about?" I asked sarcastically.

"When I couldn't find you in the castle, I knew you must have gone without me. As soon as I walked in the abandoned building, I saw *THIS* lying in the middle of the floor, and then I saw you unconscious."

She showed me my purple purse.

"We were supposed to go together. How could you?"

"First of all, that's not mine."

"Then why does is it say McKenna Monakean in big velvet letters in the inside? Huh? Explain that!"

"Um, uh, it's probably just a coincidence. There's most likely another human being with that name!" I said, hopelessly trying to convince Claire I didn't go to the library without her.

"Okay, does that other person named McKenna Monakean also have a six thousand dollar designer purse, and a tag on the inside that says, 'Please return to the royal castle if found'?"

"Possibly!"

"What were you doing there? I thought we were doing this together!"

"I'm sorry, but I found a lot of helpful information!"

"Like what?"

"I met another ghost and he claims to be a family member! He knows a lot about what's going on!"

"Like what?"

"He was telling me about someone named Jeremy Monakean."

"Monakean? As in he's related to us?" Claire asked.

"I guess. This was my first time talking to a dead ancestor who knows more about our family then me!"

"At least you didn't get hurt."

"Since when did you start caring?" I asked Claire.

"Well, uh, um," said Claire mumbling stuff under her breath. She then changed the subject and said, "When we leave this place, do you know where we're going?"

"Cookie Bake Ice Cream Parlor?"

"No. The old Linston Library, right after we stop at home!"

Chapter 8

The Findings

As we headed to the castle from the hospital, I explained everything to Claire that had happened in the library and told her about the newspaper article. We assumed that Jeremy Monakean was the King from the newspaper article because of the whispers I heard before I passed out. We walked calmly into the palace, and then both ran up to Claire's room to discuss our findings.

"Okay, so we already know that there's a ghost haunting us and it has something to do with Jeremy Monakean," Claire stated trying to make sense of the situation.

"What do we know about Jeremy?" I asked.

"Well, we already know he reigned over the kingdom, and that he went 'missing' on December 8, 1823. So far that's the only info we've got about him," Claire explained.

"Okay, let's head back out to the library," I said.

"Agreed."

"Oh, by the way, can you grab a flashlight?" I said to Claire.

"Um, why?"

"Because if we have any 'encounters' I want to be ready!"

"Oh boy. Let's go!"

We told Mom and Dad we were going to take another walk around the kingdom. We both knew that if we told them what was actually going on, it would be the equivalent of a tornado hitting the kingdom.

As we reached the old library, everything seemed the same. Claire said, "Okay, let's look around and stay on topic. That means NO PUPPET SHOWS!"

"Where am I gonna find a show of sock puppets in the middle of a creepy abandoned building?"

"That's not the point. Look for anything that could possibly be helpful."

We looked for hours and hours until suddenly I found something. "Hey look what I found!" I yelled over to Claire. "It's a book!"

"Well, duh. We're in a library. Of course it's full of books," Claire said.

"No, this book has information about Jeremy Monakean. It's a book about the old rulers of Linston. Turns out he did used to be the King."

"At least we were right about that. Let me see that book."

As Claire flipped through the pages, my mind went through all the events of the last few days. There was something odd in all of this that I couldn't place my finger on. Suddenly, Claire gasped.

"McKenna look!" she exclaimed, as she shook my shoulder back and forth aggressively. She was pointing to a picture of what appeared to be Jeremy Monakean.

"I'm looking. What's there to see?" I asked, not having a clue what Claire was talking about.

"Look in the background. Do you see anyone familiar?"

"Oh my gosh!! That looks like Henry! But how can Henry be in a book from so many years ago?"

"Yeah, you're right!" Claire said.

Suddenly, it dawned on me. Henry was the ghost. It all made sense now. He was spying on us when we were in the ballroom. There was also that big bruise on his forehead right where Claire had hit the ghost with her flashlight. Also, he had access to my room, so the first time we got haunted he was able to come in my room. I quickly explained my theory to Claire and she agreed with me. There was still so much that we didn't know. Thoughts raced through my mind.

Who is Henry? How can he be both real and a ghost? How is he involved in this? Did he knock me out? Why did he get so close to us? Why is he even haunting us?

"We should get out of here. The sun is going down. We've been here for hours," Claire said, still shocked by our discovery.

"Yeah, just stay away from Henry and act normal. Be sure to grab the book and we'll do more research at home," I said.

All of a sudden, I heard footsteps. They grew louder as they approached the door. Seconds later, when the door swung open, I felt cold air blow on my neck. It was just like what had happened at the castle. *I have a bad feeling about this* I thought. We turned around, only to see Henry. He looked angry.

Chapter 9

The Truth

"If you give me that book now, no harm will come to you," Henry said.

"No, never!" Claire said.

"Okay, I gave you a warning!"

In one swift motion, Henry came over and tried to grab the book, but Claire quickly ducked out of the way before he could.

"We know who you are!" I exclaimed. "What do you want from us?"

"You girls are smarter than I expected. I didn't think you would figure it out so soon."

"Figure out what?" I asked, as Claire and Henry were practically having a tug-of-war with the book.

"My true identity."

"I wouldn't mind a little help here," Claire muttered under her breath to me.

"Oh whoops. I forgot about you over there," I told her.

"Why are you haunting us? What did we ever do to you, huh?" I asked him.

"Not everything in life is always about you, princesses," said Henry. "I want to destroy the entire monarchy. No descendant of Jeremy Monakean should ever be in power.

Haunting you was just a small step in a bigger plan. I was foolish. I thought you could be scared out of the throne. Why do you think I got so close to you?"

"What do you have against Jeremy Monakean and his descendants?"

He chuckled bitterly and said, "I was Jeremy's personal guard back in the old days. I was nothing more than a servant to him. He treated me like a piece of trash, garbage. I finally had enough of his disrespect! I searched until I dug up a deep secret of his. When I finally confronted him, he threatened to fire me. If he did, I would never get another job again, so I took him out of the picture. Unfortunately, he showed up again the other day. He came back as a ghost too—you girls probably met him. He was the one who told you about his disappearance. He knew you would figure it out if you could just find the right book. I'm sure he wanted to protect you and the royal family throne, especially with your coronation coming up so soon."

"Who are you talking about?" I asked.

"The old guy who gave you that newspaper!"

"That was JEREMY MONAKEAN!" Claire and I both exclaimed.

"Yup," he answered, rolling his eyes.

"What about the Linston Library? Why did you tell us about that?"

"I expected the two of you to go to the library together. The green gas was supposed to get rid of you both, but then McKenna showed up alone and foiled my plans. Unfortunately for me, Claire got to you before the gas did its job."

"Enough chit chat now! Give me the book!" Henry yelled full of rage and determination.

Then Claire just started bolting out of the library as fast as she could with the book in her hand. I followed her. Henry followed as well and was not that far behind us!

"Do you have a plan?" I asked Claire as we ran.

"Nope just run as fast as you can!" Claire replied back.

We ran all throughout the town until we finally thought we lost him.

"Hey, I think he's gone. Let's take a quick stop. I'm totally out of breath," I said as we stopped near the train tracks to catch our breath.

"I have a better plan," said Henry sneaking up behind us.

We were frozen—there was nowhere to run. We were cornered. I could feel knots in my stomach.

He snatched the book from the palm of Claire's hand. Suddenly, he dropped the book, not even a second after stealing it from us. He tried to grab it again, but he dropped it. Henry quickly picked it up before either of us could. He dropped it again, but this time Claire picked it up and put it behind her back.

Then I said, "What's going on? Why can't he hold the book, but you can?"

"I knew it," he yelled.

"Knew what?"

"It's cursed. It's the last piece of information about me, so I can't touch it. Everybody else besides me can hold it. You happen to be the only people who have touched it in almost two hundred years. I can't let you reveal my real identity. Destroy it."

I heard a train coming and I think he was asking us to throw it onto the tracks.

"There is no way I'm destroying this book and erasing the only evidence of what you did to the King all those years ago," Claire said.

"Then you leave me no choice," Henry said angrily.

"What are you gonna do?" Claire said very sassily.

"What I've been wanting to do for sometime now," Henry said. He took out his phone and showed us a picture of our parents! They were sitting in a dungeon with tape on their mouths. Their hands were tied behind their back.

"Throw the book on the tracks now or I'll make your parents disappear FOR GOOD— like I have done before!" Henry said eerily.

Without hesitation Claire threw the book on the tracks immediately. A few seconds later, I saw the train zip over the book!

I looked over at Henry. He started screaming and said, "YOU FOOLS, LOOK WHAT YOU'VE DONE!"

I was really confused. Then suddenly Henry just started to fade into thin air! A few seconds later, he was gone. Disappeared. Vanished. Claire's and my jaw dropped. We were so confused! *How did Henry just disappear like that?* Then, I heard mumbling.

"Hey, what was that?" Claire asked, referring to the weird sound.

"Don't know," I said.

After the train finally past, I went with Claire to go look at the book. We both still heard mumbling. As we walked over we realized the book was still perfectly intact. It must be indestructable.

"Hello?" we both said suspiciously as we opened the book.

"I should have known!" said an angry voice coming from the book.

"HENRY?" we both yelled.

"Yup," he answered.

"How did you get in there?" Claire asked sternly.

"You sent me here," he said.

"How?" I asked.

"I was able to be both a ghost and in my human form as long as no one knew my true identity and what I had done. After you found out about me from the book, I thought destroying the book would let me live on until

I accomplished my goal of eliminating the monarchy. Now I will be trapped in the book as a part of history forever," Henry explained.

"What?" Claire said, full of surprise.

"It's where you belong" I said very angrily as I slammed the book closed and put it in my purse.

Claire gasped. "MOM AND DAD! They could be hurt!" We sprinted back to the castle as fast as we could, bringing the book with us. We burst through the doors and I yelled, "MOM! DAD! Are you guys okay?"

"Yeah," said Mom, looking at Dad and sounding very confused and angry. It was then that I realized they were in the middle of an important meeting about Claire's coronation. I felt my face getting warmer as I filled up with embarrassment.

"So you guys *weren't* kidnapped?" Claire asked very confused as well.

"What are you two talking about?" Dad asked. "We weren't kidnapped." It finally made sense! The photo Henry showed must have been a fake. He had access to lots of photos of my parents and could have easily edited them so it looked like they were kidnapped. He was trying to trick us!

"Oops," I said. I grabbed Claire's hand and pulled her out of the throne room.

"Wait," said Mom. "Claire, we need to get your dress fitted for the coronation."

"Okay," Claire said, "McKenna you go ahead and leave without me."

"Okay," I said as I left the room.

Before I left I stopped to add, "By the way Mom, Henry stopped working here because his grandmother is dying and he wanted to stay with her. He wanted to let you know he was sorry for leaving so suddenly. He also wanted us to pass along the message." I lied, not knowing what else to do.

"Oh, we give our best wishes to his grandma," Mom said.

"You should get ready for the coronation, you know. It's next week. You want to be prepared," Dad said.

"Okay," I said. As I left the room, I rushed outside and buried the book deep on castle property where no one would ever find it. Henry will never be heard from again.

Epilogue

Today is the day. The day of Claire's coronation. Everyone is rushing throughout the palace. It's so hectic! As I walked upstairs to put on my gown, I heard crying. It was coming from Claire's room! *Why is Claire upset? This is her big day!*

"What's wrong?" I asked very concerned. "Is it about Henry?"

"No, it's that—I don't think I'm ready to be Queen. It's too soon. I need more time to study the kingdom, learn the rules, and—"

I cut her off. "Trust me! You're gonna be great! Besides today's your coronation, a celebration of you and no one but you! Don't worry about all the other stuff and celebrate how you are going to be the best Queen of Linston. With a five star rated sidekick! I'm you're Q.U.I.T. Queen In Training! It has a nice ring to it!" I told her.

"What does the U stand for?"

"I'm still working out the details," I said.

"I think I'm ready," she said proudly.

In my head I wanted to say, *Finally, I've knocked some sense into you*, but since it was Claire's coronation I decided to be nice and say, "You can do this! Your Quitter is by your side." Claire exited the room laughing!

As I entered the ballroom, I sat down at the table with the other members of the Linston royal family. All of my family was there—it was like a huge family reunion! As Claire walked up to the podium, she seemed very nervous.

She looked at me and I gave her the "You'll Be Perfectly Fine" face. She smiled and said, "I am Claire Monakean, the new ruler of Linston. I will do my best to support your needs and listen to your suggestions. I will help keep our kingdom safe. I will help improve the economy. I will make Linston a better place to live."

For the next few minutes, she talked about her agenda as Queen. When she was done with her speech, the applause was gigantic! Everyone loved her! They placed the crown on her head with great honor. I was really happy for Claire. Amazingly, all the shenanigans actually brought us closer together. I know we won't ever be perfect or even normal sisters, but I do know that we've got each other's back and that won't change!

SIGMA'S BOOKSHELF

Sigma's Bookshelf (www.SigmasBookshelf.com) is an independent book publishing company that exclusively publishes the work of teenage authors, who are between the ages of 13 - 19. The company was founded in 2016 by Minnesota teenager Justin M. Anderson, whose first book, *Saving Stripes: A Kitty's Story*, was published when he was 14, and has since sold hundreds of copies.

"I know there are a lot of other teenagers out there who are good writers and deserve to have their work published, but don't have access to the kinds of resources I do. I wanted to help them," he said.

Sigma's Bookshelf is a sponsored project of Springboard for the Arts, a nonprofit arts service organization. Contributions on behalf of Sigma's Bookshelf may be made payable to Springboard for the Arts and are tax deductible to the extent permitted by law. Donations can be made online at www.SigmasBookshelf.com/donate.

www.ingramcontent.com/pod-product-compliance
Lightning Source LLC
Chambersburg PA
CBHW020624120726
47905CB00003B/932